A Tale of Two Cities

Charles Dickens

SADDLEBACK
EDUCATIONAL PUBLISHING

Saddleback's *Illustrated Classics*™

SADDLEBACK
EDUCATIONAL PUBLISHING
www.sdlback.com

ISBN-13: 978-1-56254-940-4
ISBN-10: 1-56254-940-5
eBook: 978-1-60291-169-7

Printed in Guangzhou, China
0611/CA21100673

16 15 14 13 12   4 5 6 7 8

Welcome to
Saddleback's *Illustrated Classics*™

We are proud to welcome you to Saddleback's *Illustrated Classics*™. Saddleback's *Illustrated Classics*™ was designed specifically for the classroom to introduce readers to many of the great classics in literature. Each text, written and adapted by teachers and researchers, has been edited using the Dale-Chall vocabulary system. In addition, much time and effort has been spent to ensure that these high-interest stories retain all of the excitement, intrigue, and adventure of the original books.

With these graphically *Illustrated Classics*™, you learn what happens in the story in a number of different ways. One way is by reading the words a character says. Another way is by looking at the drawings of the character. The artist can tell you what kind of person a character is and what he or she is thinking or feeling.

This series will help you to develop confidence and a sense of accomplishment as you finish each novel. The stories in Saddleback's *Illustrated Classics*™ are fun to read. And remember, fun motivates!

Overview

Everyone deserves to read the best literature our language has to offer. Saddleback's *Illustrated Classics*™ was designed to acquaint readers with the most famous stories from the world's greatest authors, while teaching essential skills. You will learn how to:

- Establish a purpose for reading
- Activate prior knowledge
- Evaluate your reading
- Listen to the language as it is written
- Extend literary and language appreciation through discussion and writing activities.

Reading is one of the most important skills you will ever learn. It provides the key to all kinds of information. By reading the *Illustrated Classics*™, you will develop confidence and the self-satisfaction that comes from accomplishment—a solid foundation for any reader.

Step-By-Step

The following is a simple guide to using and enjoying each of your *Illustrated Classics*™. To maximize your use of the learning activities provided, we suggest that you follow these steps:

1. ***Listen!*** We suggest that you listen to the read-along. (At this time, please ignore the beeps.) You will enjoy this wonderfully dramatized presentation.

2. ***Post-reading Activities.*** You have successfully read the story and listened to the audio presentation. Now answer the multiple-choice questions and other activities in the Study Guide.

Remember,

"Today's readers are tomorrow's leaders."

Charles Dickens

Charles Dickens, perhaps the most popular and greatest English novelist of all time, was born in 1812, the son of a clerk in the Navy-Pay office. Although from a poor background and forced to go to work at the age of 10, he was still both ambitious and industrious. His education came on his own through books—those in school as well as his own.

Dickens wrote of people as he saw them, and because of his concern for social conditions in England, created some of the most memorable, timeless characters in literature. At 31 years old, in order to pay some pressing debts, he wrote *A Christmas Carol*, a wonderful, intriguing, joyful mystery about the spirit of Christmas, and without question one of the most widely read classics of all time. The particular characters Dickens created for this story—Scrooge, Bob Cratchit, Tiny Tim, and the Ghosts of Christmas—will always remain indelibly etched in literature.

The turning point in his life came at the time of his marriage. Both his wedding day and his first publication occurred in the same year. Some of his other timeless stories such as *A Tale of Two Cities, Oliver Twist*, and *Great Expectations* were immensely popular in Victorian England; however, it is said that *A Christmas Carol* is his finest accomplishment.

Dickens, surely one of the greatest storytellers and creators of memorable characters, died in 1870.

Charles Dickens

A Tale of
Two Cities

Dr. Manette

Charles
Darnay

Sydney
Carton

Madame
Defarge

Mr. Lorry

Miss Pross

Lucie Manette

Monsieur Defarge

Until the year 1775, the kings of both France and England ruled with great power. But they did not rule kindly or fairly, and people all over were dying from hunger. At last the peasants of France, some 300,000 in number, joined together to overthrow the King. They captured him, tried him, found him guilty, and had him beheaded.

"It was the best of times,
it was the worst of times,
it was the age of wisdom,
it was the age of foolishness,
it was the season of Light,
it was the season of Darkness,
it was the spring of hope,
it was the season of despair."

It is at this time that our story takes place . . . set in the cities of Paris and London . . . the people are some of the innocent and some of the guilty who were alive at that time.

One winter day in 1775, the mail coach from London finished its journey to Dover.

Welcome, sir! A room?

Will there a boat to Calais tomorrow?

Yes, sir, if the weather holds.

Then I wish a room for myself—and one for a young lady who will arrive shortly.

She may ask for me by name—Lorry—or she may ask for the man from Tellson's Bank.

A little later . . .

Miss Manette has arrived, sir.

So soon?

The Bank writes there is news about my poor dead father—that I must go to Paris. May I go with you?

I would be pleased, Ma'am.

They said you would have surprising news for me and that you would explain.

Well . . . it is hard to begin.

Twenty years ago in Paris, I did some work for a Frenchman, a famous doctor . . . Dr. Manette.

My father!

He married an English lady, and I was one of his lawyers.

My mother outlived my father by only two years— then I was left an orphan. . . .

Was it you who brought me to England?

It was I. And now suppose— that your father had not died!

Suppose he had been taken away by an enemy— that he had been secretly put in prison. . . .

That his wife had begged the King and the court for news of him, but she never was answered.

The truth— I beg you!

My dear, he has been found. He is alive!

It will be his ghost!

No! Greatly changed, worn out, but alive, and taken to the house of an old servant in Paris.

We will go to him there—I to prove who he is, and you to bring him back to life!

In the St. Antoine area of Paris, on a narrow, dirty street, was the wine shop of M. and Mme. Defarge. Mr. Lorry took Lucie there upon their arrival in Paris.

M. Defarge?

Sit down. My husband will be here soon.

M. Defarge entered the shop smiling, open-faced.

Good day. May I help you?

We came to see Dr. Manette.

He led them into an apartment, up a steep, dark, dirty staircase with garbage on every landing.

Best to start slowly. It is five flights up.

When he learned who Mr. Lorry was, he was changed instantly into an angry man.

This way, please.

He stopped at the door of an attic room and took out a key.

Possible? Yes. And many other such things are possible, and done—done! Every day!

He has lived so long locked up, he would be afraid if the door were left open.

Is it possible?

One would have said the attic room was too dark for work; yet a man sat on a low bench, very busy making shoes.

Good day.

You have a visitor.

Dr. Manette, do you remember me?

For a second it looked as if he might remember.

Then darkness fell again. With a deep sigh, he returned to work.

Do you know him?

Yes. For a moment I saw the face I once knew!

He learned shoemaking in prison. He knows nothing else, not even his name, and calls himself by his cell number.

What is your name, sir?

105, North Tower.

Lucie stepped near Dr. Manette.

What—who are you?

Oh, sir! Oh, my dear!

That voice—this golden hair—the same as . . . But no, you are too young, how can it be? What is your name, my gentle angel?

At another time you shall know my name.

For now, believe me that your pain is over! I have come to take you to England to be at peace and at rest.

So, by coach and by ship, Dr. Manette was taken to London. Slowly, Lucie's tender care brought him back to health. They lived quietly and happily in a pleasant house just off Soho square, where Dr. Manette's medical knowledge and skill brought him many patients.

Five years passed. Then, in 1780, there was great excitement in London over the trial for treason of Charles Darnay, a young Frenchman.

The prisoner was charged with traveling between England and France to give English secrets to the French King.

The court's lawyer claimed that the proof went back as far as five years. Miss Lucie Manette was called as a witness.

Yes, Mr. Darnay was aboard ship when I brought my ill father from France to London.

He was very kind and gentle and helped to care for my father. I hope I do him no harm today.

The court's lawyer called another witness, a man who was once a servant of Darnay's.

My master often traveled between France and England.

I saw important looking lists and papers in his pockets and in his desk.

Sometimes I saw him show such lists to Frenchmen!

Darnay's lawyer said that his travels were on personal business. Then he asked the servant questions.

Weren't you angry because Mr. Darnay had fired you—for stealing a silver coffee pot?

No, sir! Never!

It was only a little pitcher—and not real silver.

Ha!

Another witness said that he had seen Darnay collecting information near a military post.

Are you quite sure it was the prisoner?

Quite sure!

Look at the gentleman, my assistant. Then look at the prisoner.

The assistant, Sydney Carton, rose and removed his white wig.

Not only the witness, but everyone present, was surprised by the likeness. The jury found Charles Darnay innocent, and he was released. His friends gathered to congratulate him.

As father and daughter left, Sydney Carton walked up to Darnay.

It was strange chance that threw us together. Shall we dine together at the nearest tavern?

Yes, and I owe you thanks for your help today!

I hardly seem to belong to this world again.

My greatest desire is to forget that I belong to it. It has no good in it for me—except wine like this!

I care for no man on earth, and no man cares for me.

That is too bad.

Maybe so. Don't look so happy. You don't know what may come later.

Good night!

Left alone, Carton picked up a candle and went to a mirror on the wall.

Ah! Do you like what you see?

Say it plainly! You hate the fellow—for showing what you once were, and what you might have been.

He returned to his wine, drank it all in a few minutes, and fell asleep on his arms.

Charles Darnay made his home in England, as a teacher of the French language. A part of his time was spent at Cambridge teaching university students. But family business still forced him to make visits to France.

There, while the people starved, the King and his friends lived as if life were an endless, fancy ball.

Quickly driving through the narrow streets, the rich seemed to enjoy watching the common people jump to escape being run down.

Watch out!

One day as the carriage of the Marquis St. Evremonde swept round a corner, it hit something and the horses reared.

Why can't you take care of your children? I don't know what injury you have done to my horses.

The Marquis tossed a gold coin from the window.

Here. Give him that.

Suddenly the coin flew back through the window.

Wait! Who threw that?

You dogs! I would ride over any of you willingly and wipe you from the earth.

At sunset, the Marquis arrived at his country estate. Waiting for him was his nephew. Known in England as Charles Darnay, he was the son of the dead twin brother of the Marquis.

You have taken a long time to return.

I only return because I must!

Our family hurts everyone who comes between us and our wishes. Our name is the most hated in France!

It is only natural they should hate us.

I am stuck with a way of life I hate! If this property were mine I would give it up, as I have given up France.

28

It is not yet yours! For myself, I will die to protect my power and property!

What is that noise? Open the blinds.

There is nothing here.

Very well. Now I will say good night.

Good night, sir.

Later, as the Marquis slept. . . .

The father of the dead child had his revenge.

Charles Darnay returned to London. There, like a ship safely in harbor after a stormy voyage, Dr. Manette lived in peace with Lucie. The good Miss Pross, with whom Lucie had lived while she was an orphan, was a part of the household. And their friends were always welcome there.

Mr. Lorry, Charles Darnay, and Sydney Carton visited often.

How cool and pleasant it is here.

Not a quieter spot in London.

One day Darnay called when he knew he would find Dr. Manette alone.

Charles Darnay! I am happy to see you.

I wish to speak with you, sir. . . .

I love your daughter with all my heart. I wish to marry her.

I am not surprised!

Have you spoken of this to Lucie?

No, never.

If Lucie should tell me that she needs you for her happiness, I will give her to you.

Thank you, sir!

I must tell you my real name—and why I am in England.

No, stop!

If Lucie loves you, if you marry her, you shall tell me on your wedding day. Not before!

And so it was that Charles Darnay asked Lucie to marry him.

It is with your father's permission that I ask!

Dear Charles, yes!

Soon after it was another man, Sydney Carton, who spoke to Lucie of love.

I do not ask for your love Miss Manette—nor even want it. I am a wasted man who would pull you down with me.

Even without it, can I not help you? Oh, Mr. Carton, think again! Try again!

It is too late. I ask only that you will think kindly of me in your heart.

I will, Mr. Carton, always.

For you, and any dear to you, I would do anything. I would give my life to keep a life you love beside you. God bless you!

The wedding day arrived. Behind the closed door of Dr. Manette's room, Darnay talked with him.

Doctor, it is my mother's name I use. I am truly the Marquis St. Evremonde.

Dr. Manette's face turned pale.

You say . . . St. Evremonde?

Yes . . . is something wrong?

No, no. Go on.

I have given up my rights. I have left my property in the hands of an employee, to be used for the people.

I earn my own living by my own labor.

Yes, I see.

I ask one thing: promise me you will never tell anyone else your true name.

I promise you, sir.

And so Lucie and Charles were married.

Take her, Charles! She is yours!

In Paris, an Englishman, an old friend, came to the Defarge's shop to drink wine.

It was you who cared for Dr. Manette when he was released.

That is true. . . .

Do you know his daughter has married a Frenchman?

No. . . .

He is called Darnay in England, but he is truly the Marquis St. Evremonde!

If it is true, I hope for her sake Fate will keep her husband out of France.

Her husband's luck will take him where he is to go, and will lead him to the end that is to end him!

In London, Darnay and Lucie lived happily with Dr. Manette. A daughter, little Lucie, lived with them.

Late on a night in mid-July, 1789, Mr. Lorry came to the Darnay's from Tellson's Bank.

It was July 14. Paris had become like a whirlpool of boiling water. Someone was giving out weapons.

The center of the whirlpool was Defarge's wine shop.

Let's separate and all lead as many men as we can.

And you, my wife?

Defarge! I will lead the women! We can kill as well as the men!

Come then! We are ready! To the Bastille!

With a roar of anger, with alarm bells ringing, drums beating, the crowd attacked the Bastille—the state-prison in Paris, most hated by the people.

The white flag of surrender appeared. The mob swept over the lowered drawbridge into the courtyard, Defarge leading.

Free the prisoners! Go to the secret cells!

You! Take me to 105, North Tower.

In the cell, Defarge examined the walls.

Pass that torch along these walls.

A.M.! Dr. Alexandre Manette! This is it!

Finding a crowbar, he turned to the chimney.

They are here—the papers!

Once begun, the revolution swept over France and became a time of terror. Treated badly for too long, the common people turned upon the King and his friends hurting the innocent along with the guilty. Many rich people fled to England.

Their meeting place in London was Tellson's Bank. There, in August, 1792, Charles Darnay talked to Mr. Lorry.

Must you go to Paris, sir? The city may not be safe.

My dear, Charles, it is safe enough for me.

It is you Frenchmen who stand in danger of being beheaded!

It is very important for the bank that I go, and go tonight!

By the way, here is a letter secretly brought to us from France, but I can't locate the person to whom it should go.

Let me see it.

It was addressed to himself! But Darnay remembered his promise to Dr. Manette not to tell his name.

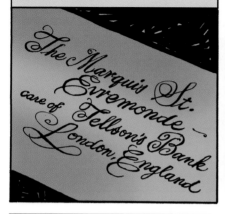

I know him. I will deliver it. And good luck on your journey.

Goodbye, Charles.

Later, Darnay read the letter.

Abbaye Prison, Paris
June 21, 1792

Monsieur the Marquis:

I have been seized and imprisoned and shall lose my life, without your help! I am accused of acting against the people for an emigrant. In vain I say I have acted for the people, according to your commands. They say I have acted for an emigrant, and where is that emigrant? I beg you to return and release me. I have been true to you, Sir, I pray you to be true to me.
Your unhappy servant
Gabelle

Poor Gabelle! I should not have left him alone to handle things. In my happiness here, I have forgotten my duties in France. I must go to Paris.

I will explain to Lucie and her father in letters to be delivered after I leave. It will keep them from having to say sad goodbyes.

Reaching France, Darnay found things worse than he had expected. Every town gate had its citizen-guards who stopped all those who tried to pass through.

I want to go to Paris!

Emigrant. I am going to send you to Paris with a guard.

In Paris, he was taken before an officer of the people, Citizen Defarge.

You are the emigrant Evremonde?

I am no emigrant, and I am in France of my own free will!

Why, in the name of that sharp thing you called La Guillotine, did you return to France?

You will be held in La Force prison.

We have new laws since you were here.

But have I not the right to . . .

Under what law?

Emigrants have no rights.

A few days later, as Mr. Lorry worked in the Paris office of Tellson's Bank, his door burst open.

Lucie! Dr. Manette! What has brought you here?

Charles is here! An act of kindness brought him, unknown to us. He was stopped at the barrier and sent to La Force prison.

La Force!

My dears, don't worry. I am a Bastille prisoner. Any fighter in France will help me! I know I can help Charles out of danger.

If that is so, act quickly! There is no time to waste! I will keep the others here.

Mr. Lorry knew though the others did not, that even at that moment mobs were putting the rich into prisons and killing them by the hundreds.

But Dr. Manette was right. As soon as he made himself known, the crowd took him to its heart and set out to help him.

Make way for the Bastille prisoner! Help the Bastille prisoner's relative. Save the prisoner Evremonde at La Force!

At La Force, he was taken before a committee that was trying the prisoners. One of its members was Defarge. He knew the doctor.

My son-in-law is a prisoner here. I beg you for his life and liberty.

We cannot release him, but we will keep him in safety.

Dr. Manette!

I am going to stay with you—to see that no harm or bad luck finds you turned over to the mob outside!

For four days Dr. Manette stayed with Charles. The next night he was able to send Lucie a note from Charles.

Monsieur Defarge, I believe? And Madame!

Yes, I come from Dr. Manette. I bring a message.

Dearest--
Take courage.
I am well, and your
father protects me.
Kiss our child.

He is safe! Oh, thank you, Madame!

Is that Evremonde's child?

Come, Defarge. I have seen them. We may go.

After the Defarges left. . . .

That woman seems to throw a shadow on me and all my hopes.

The worst danger over, Dr. Manette returned. Fifteen months passed. During all that time Lucie was never sure, from hour to hour, whether the guillotine would strike off her husband's head next day.

At long last, Charles Darnay was brought to Court. For a second time he stood on trial for his life.

Darnay noticed only two faces in the crowd:

a hard faced woman . . .

. . . and his kind father-in-law.

You are being accused of being an emigrant, under the law which says all emigrants must stay out of the country forever under . . .

I do not think of myself as an emigrant, sir.

Have you not lived many years in England?

Yes, sir.

By my own wish I gave up a title and I position I disliked, and went to England to live by my own labors, rather than staying to live on the labors of the people of France!

Did you not marry in England?

True, but I married a French woman.

Her name and family?

Lucie Manette, only daughter of Dr. Manette, the good doctor who sits there.

Darnay was asked why he had returned to France when he did, and Gabelle, who had been freed a few days earlier, spoke for him.

It is true—I wrote and begged him to return to save me!

Then Dr. Manette was questioned.

Darnay has been faithful to my daughter and myself in our exile.

We have had enough. We are ready to vote.

Every vote was in Darnay's favor.

Charles Darnay, I declare you free!

In a wild, dreamlike parade the crowd carried Darnay home on its shoulders. So, at last, he was back with his family.

Lucie! My own! I am safe.

Now speak to your father. No other man in all France could have done what he has done for me!

Oh, father!

My dear, I am thankful.

But that evening there was a knock on the door.

What can this be! Hide Charles. Save him!

My child, I have saved him. Let me go to the door.

Four armed men in red caps entered the room.

We come to arrest the citizen Evremonde, called Darnay.

How and why am I again a prisoner?

You have been accused by the Section of St. Antoine.

By citizen and citizeness Defarge— and one other.

What other?

Do you ask, citizen Doctor?

Yes.

Then you will be answered at the trial tomorrow.

Sydney Carton had just arrived in Paris and was worried about his friends.

I have bad news. Darnay has been arrested again.

But I left him safe and free only a few hours ago!

I learned of his arrest from a prison spy who owes me something.

Can this man help?

He hasn't much power. But if the trial goes badly, I can make one visit to Darnay in his cell.

Leaving, Carton made his way to a small chemist's shop.

You know the danger if you mix these?

I know.

During the night, knowing he would not sleep, Sydney Carton walked the streets of Paris. He remembered his mother who died in his childhood. He remembered his father's funeral. He walked with purpose, like a man who had found his road and saw its end.

At dawn he stood on a bridge over the river. He watched the stars fade, the sun rise. He remembered the words spoken over his father's grave.

"I am the resurrection and the life; he that believeth in me, though dead, yet shall he live. . . ."

That morning, again, Darnay was brought to trial.

Charles Evremonde, you are an accused enemy of the French Republic, one of a family of cruel leaders who should die.

Who does the accusing?

Ernest Defarge. Therese Defarge, his wife.

And one other, Alexandre Manette, the doctor.

Pale and trembling, Dr. Manette rose.

I protest to you that this is a lie! Who and where is the man who says that I accuse the husband of my child?

Citizen, listen to what follows, In the meantime, be silent.

Defarge spoke. He told of Dr. Manette's imprisonment, of his release, of the Defarge's care of him. He told of the fall of the Bastille, of his visit to cell 105, North Tower; of the hole in the chimney, and the written papers he found there.

These are the papers I found. This is the writing of Dr. Manette.

Let the papers be read.

I, Alexandre Manette, write this sad paper in my Bastille cell, in the last month of 1767.

I swear that I write the truth. Someone may find it when I and my sorrows are dust.

One night in December, 1757, as I walked by the river, a fast-driven carriage came up behind. I stood aside, but instead of passing, it stopped.

Stop, driver!

Two young men got out. They looked like twin brothers.

You are Dr. Manette?

I am.

Please enter my carriage.

They were armed. I had no choice. I entered and was driven to a lonely country house.

Your patient is upstairs, doctor.

The patient was a beautiful young woman. She was out of her head.

My husband, my father, my brother!

She has a high fever of the brain.

My husband, my father, my brother!

I fear there is little to do for her.

Very well. There is another patient.

In a loft over a stable, the young woman's brother lay dying of a sword wound.

How did this happen?

He is a common farmer. He forced my brother to draw his sword, and fell by it, like a gentleman.

The boy was dying. He told me his story.

We rented farm land from the Marquis. We were taxed without mercy, worked without mercy, worked without pay. We were robbed and hunted and starved.

They worked my sister's husband to death. Then they took her to the Chateau. My father died of sorrow.

I took my younger sister to safety. Then I came here. Now I die, too.

With a great effort, the boy raised himself.

Marquis, in the days when these crimes will be answered for, I call you and all your family to answer for them!

So the boy died; and shortly afterward, his sister.

Returning home, I wrote a letter to the police telling them the truth of what had happened. But my letter never reached them.

So! You would have told my secret to the police! You will pay for this!

So I was brought to my living grave.

The name of these brothers was Evremonde. I denounce them and their descendants, to the last of their race. I denounce them to Heaven and to Earth.

When the document was finished, a great cry for blood arose in the Court. Every juryman voted "guilty."

To the guillotine!

Guilty!

Guilty!

Guilty!

For you, Charles Evremonde, enemy of the people, death within twenty-four hours!

As Darnay was led away . . .

I beg your forgiveness.

Never kneel to me! I know what you felt when you learned my name. With all my heart I thank you for all you have done for me.

But Sydney Carton had made his plans. He went to Defarge's wine shop.

An Englishman—but how like Evremonde!

They were still excited about the trial.

Evremonde is done for, but his wife, and the child—they too must be killed!

We must stop somewhere.

The farm family so hurt by the Evremondes was my family! That boy was my brother. That girl was my sister. That father was my father!

Those dead are my dead!

Tell the Wind and the Fire to stop; not me!

Carton went next to Mr. Lorry's.

My bench—where is it? I must finish my shoes.

Poor fellow! The shock was too much for him.

Carton told what he heard at the wine shop . . . that Lucie and the child were in danger, that Madame Defarge planned to have them killed.

You must take Dr. Manette, Lucie, and the child back to London tomorrow—while their passes to leave are still good.

It shall be done!

Take my pass. Bring the Manettes and meet me outside the prison gates at two o'clock tomorrow. When I come, take me in and drive away for London.

Promise that when my place in the coach is filled, you will let nothing stop you!

I promise.

The following day, in Darnay's cell . . .

Carton! How—why are you here?

Never mind! Take off your boots and put on mine.

There is no escaping from here—it's madness!

As Darnay removed his coat, Carton knocked him out with the drug he had bought.

In a moment, Darnay was out cold. Carton quickly finished changing their clothing, then called the prison spy.

Tell the guards he fainted while saying goodbye to me. Have him carried to Mr. Lorry's carriage below.

In a short time, Mr. Lorry's coach was leaving the city.

You have your passes?

Yes.

Dr. Alexandre Manette; his daughter Lucie; a child Lucie; Mr. Lorry, banker, English; Sydney Carton, English—Mr. Carton is not well?

He will recover in the fresh air.

The coach passed through in safely.

Depart, citizens!

In the meantime, Madame Defarge made plans of her own.

Evremonde dies today, but his wife and child still live. Are they not also Evremondes?

Yes! They too must die.

I will go to them now to find them crying over the death of Evremonde. That too is a crime you know. . . .

. . . and punishable by death.

Alone in the apartment, Miss Pross was getting ready to follow her dear friends in another coach, when Madame Defarge appeared at the door.

The wife and child of Evremonde; where are they?

If only I can give my darlings some more time to get out of Paris.

You shall not see them as long as I can stop you, you evil woman!

Idiot! Let me by!

From the folds of her skirt, Madame Defarge drew a pistol. They fought briefly, and . . .

A few minutes later, Miss Pross was on her way out of Paris.

As Lucie, Charles, and the others made their way back to England, Sydney Carton was on his way to the guillotine.

You are not Evremonde! Why do you die for him?

For his wife and child.

If he could have written his thoughts, Sydney Carton would have said: "I see a beautiful city and beautiful people rising from the evil of this time. In England, I see the lives for which I lay down my life, peaceful, and happy. I see myself held in the memory in their hearts, and honored in their souls."

They said, that night, that his was the most peaceful face ever seen on that platform.

It is a far, far better thing that I do, than I have ever done; it is a far, far better rest that I go to, than I have even known.

The End